CUENTO DE LUZ

To Nacho and Mariela, my brother and sister, and my cousins Martín, Pato, Silvina and Sol.

- Ariel Andrés Almada -

To my father, for being the light in my darkness.

- Zuzanna Celej -

The Lighthouse of Souls

Text © Ariel Andrés Almada
Illustrations © Zuzanna Celej
This edition © 2014 Cuento de Luz SL
Calle Claveles 10 | Urb Monteclaro | Pozuelo de Alarcón | 28223 | Madrid | Spain
www.cuentodeluz.com
Original title in Spanish: El faro de las almas
English translation by Jon Brokenbrow

ISBN: 978-84-16147-30-4

Printed by Shanghai Chenxi Printing Co., Ltd. August 2014, print number 1454-4

FSC
www.fsc.org
MIX
Paper from
responsible sources
FSC® C007923

WRITTEN BY

ARIEL A. ALMADA

ILLUSTRATED BY

ZUZANNA CELEJ

THE
LIGHTHOUSE
OF
SOULS

On their birthday, most children receive gifts like storybooks, rag dolls, colored pencils, and maybe, if they've been very good, a bike. But on Leo's ninth birthday, his grandpa gave him nothing less than an old, weather beaten lighthouse.

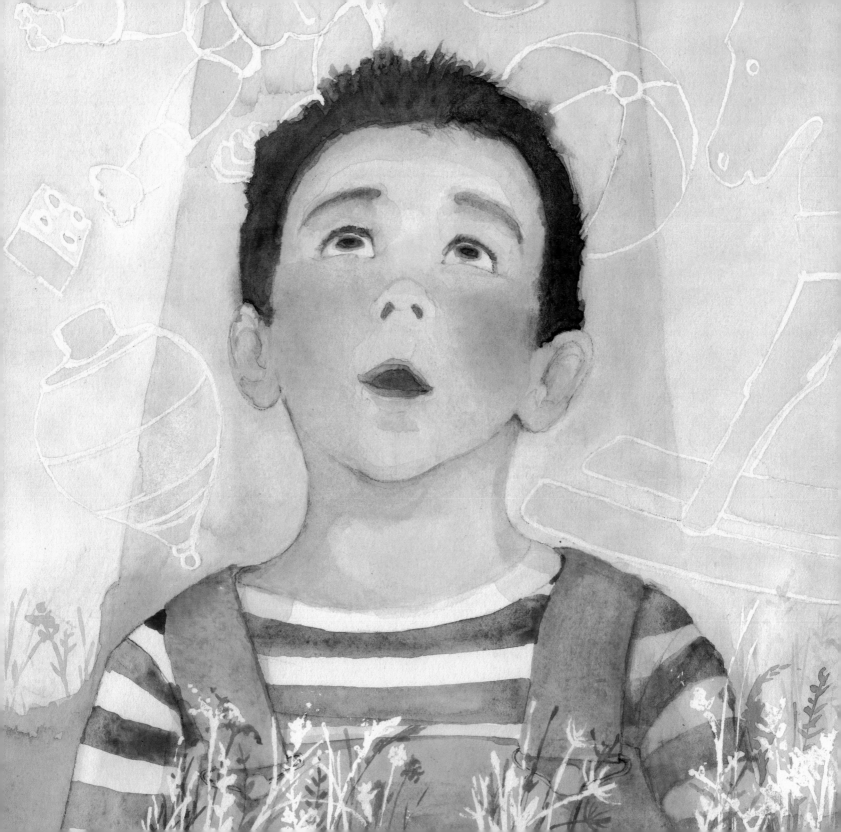

"What's a lighthouse for?" asked Leo, as they climbed up the path along the cliffs on the seashore.

"A long, long time ago, it helped to stop ships from running aground onto the rocks," said his grandpa, stroking his long beard. "But in recent years I've been using it for something quite different. Now that the lighthouse is yours, you'll need to listen very carefully to what I'm going to tell you tonight."

By the time they reached the top of the cliff, the sun had gone down and the first stars were starting to twinkle in the sky.

Leo's grandpa turned on the lantern in the lighthouse, watching carefully as it swept from left to right along the horizon, and making sure that everything was working properly. Then, he began to do something very strange indeed. First, he put his hands together and made the shape of a bird, projecting its shadow onto the clouds in the sky.

"Look Leo! It's just like a swallow! It reminds us that all of the things we miss with all our heart always come back, just like the swallows in the springtime." Then the old man wiggled his fingers, making the shadow's wings move.

Leo looked at him a little doubtfully, without really understanding what his grandpa was doing. But he seemed so enthusiastic that Leo didn't want to say anything. Then his grandpa began to switch the lantern on and off. First with three short flashes, then a long flash, and then two long flashes, as he calmly puffed away on his pipe with a big smile on his face.

"And now, my beloved grandson, it's my favorite time of the night!" he said, and began to blow huge clouds of smoke from his pipe out the window, until they covered the whole sky over the sea. "Quick, Leo! Bring me that wooden box in the corner!"

Leo brought it over, and his grandpa began to pull out a series of transparent sheets with brightly colored pictures on them.

"You're going to show a movie on the clouds!" shouted Leo, grinning from ear to ear. Finally he was beginning to feel just as excited as his grandpa.

"And this isn't just any old movie," said the old man,
with just as big a smile on his face. "Every night
it's a different story, and tonight it's an adventure
about pirates who fall in love with lost mermaids.
So get ready, because we're about to begin..."

When his grandpa finally turned off the lantern in the lighthouse,
it was nearly dawn, and the sun was starting to warm up the snails
on the rocks at the seashore. As they carefully climbed down
the cliff, Leo's grandpa whispered...

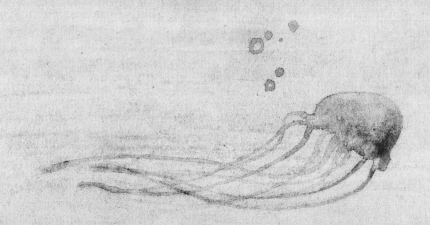

"Do you remember the shadow of the swallow I made with my hands?"

"That was for all of the fishermen's wives, who stay awake at night worrying, until they see the boats on the horizon heading back home. Our little game is to remind them that they'll soon be back together with their husbands."

"What about when you were turning the lantern on and off?" asked Leo.

"That's Morse code! All of the seafarers know it. Every night I tell a story to cheer up old Monty, who lives alone on an island five miles out to sea. Since he stopped working at sea, he's always grumpy."

"So do you do this every night, Grandpa?" asked Leo, absolutely amazed.

"I do. I come here after the sun has set to help people who are lost and just need to feel a little hope, a little encouragement, or to hear a little story to help them get through the night."

"Like the movie you projected onto the smoke from your pipe," said Leo.

"Exactly, just like that movie," said his grandpa, turning around to look for the last time at what had once been his lighthouse.

Leo and his grandpa walked together in silence along the path that wound its way down to the village.

When they reached Leo's house, his grandpa gave him a hug, enveloping him in the salty smell of the sea, reminding him that from now on, he was in charge of turning on the lantern and telling stories.

Then his grandpa slowly took off his sailor's cap, and put it on the little boy's head.

He winked at him, and then slowly
walked off down the street, whistling
a song as old as the wind.